Fix It, Please

by Ellen Weiss

Illustrated by Bill Morrison

A SESAME STREET/GOLDEN PRESS BOOK
Published by Western Publishing Company, Inc.
in conjunction with Children's Television Workshop.

It was a beautiful Monday morning on Sesame Street.
Luis was late for work.

"Today," Luis thought, "I'm finally going to fix my clock. Without it, I never know when it's time to open the Fix-It Shop. I can't wait to start working on it."

"Luis! Wait a second, Luis," called a familiar voice. Luis turned to look. Big Bird was running toward him.

"Oh, I'm so glad you're opening your shop," puffed Big Bird. "My goose-neck lamp is broken, Luis. Will you fix it, please?"

"Well, Big Bird, I was going to work on my clock today. Could you bring your lamp in tomorrow?"

"Gee...I guess so," said Big Bird, "but I'm reading *The Mystery Of The Missing Birdseed* and I'm about to find out who took the birdseed. I want to finish reading it in my nest tonight—so I need my lamp!"

Luis laughed. "Okay, Big Bird, I'll take a look at it. Come back this afternoon."

Luis had just sat down at his workbench and started to work on Big Bird's lamp when Cookie Monster charged into the shop.

"Terrible thing happened, Luis!" he moaned. "Me broke cookie jar. Me have no place to keep cookies!"

Luis sighed. "Okay, leave your cookie jar here," he said, "and come back this afternoon."

"Well," Luis thought. "I guess I can do my clock later."

As soon as Cookie Monster left, there was a knock on the door. It was Ernie.

"Hi, Ernie. What's up?" asked Luis.

"Boy, I'm glad you're here," Ernie said. "I was just going roller skating, and this little part on my skate got bent. Can you fix it, please? Right now? Huh, Luis?"

Before Luis could answer, they heard a loud noise.
SQUEAK...SQUEAK...SQUEAK!
"What can that be?" said Ernie as he and Luis
ran to the door.
"It is I, lovable, furry old Grover!" said a voice.
"What's that awful noise?" asked Luis.
"It is my little red wagon," panted Grover. "I left it
out in the rain and it got all rusted. I am so sad. Can you
fix it, please, Luis?"

"I'll fix your wagon, Grover, right after I fix Ernie's skate," Luis said. "You go play with Ernie and come back a little later."

Luis sat down and sighed a big sigh. On his workbench were the lamp, the cookie jar, the roller skate, and the little red wagon.

He wondered if he would ever get to fix his clock.

"Hi, Luis!" said Maria from the doorway. "Oscar asked if you could stop by his can for a minute to do him a favor."

Luis sighed again. "Okay," he said.

"Muchas gracias, Luis...and I think you'd better bring a hammer."

Oscar was a *very* grouchy Grouch.

"What's the matter, Oscar?" asked Luis.

"It's my dumb garbage can," complained Oscar.
"It won't slam right. It just closes with this quiet little
thud instead of a loud clang!"

"We can fix that in a minute," said Luis. "I'll just
bang it out of shape again." He began to bang the lid
with his hammer.

"There!" said Luis, giving the lid one last bang.

"Gee, thanks, Luis," said Oscar.

CLANG! Oscar disappeared, happily slamming his can lid behind him.

"Aaaah…music to my ears!" Luis heard Oscar say from inside the can.

On his way back to the Fix-It Shop, Luis passed
Mr. Hooper's store.
    "Aha! Just the person I wanted to see!" called Mr. Hooper.
"Would you fix the broken stool in my store, Luis?"
    "Oh, I guess so," answered Luis.

Martha was waiting for Luis when he got back
to his shop. She held out a broken jack-in-the-box.
"Please fix it, Luis?" she asked in a sad voice.
Luis could not say no.

Luis finished repairing the jack-in-the-box.

"All fixed! Thank you!" Martha said happily as she scampered away.

Then Herry Monster brought in his rocking chair with the broken seat.

And Prairie Dawn brought in her portable radio.
The little metal tab that held the battery in place
was broken.

Luis worked very hard to finish all the things he had promised to fix.
He looked inside Big Bird's lamp.
He finished gluing Cookie Monster's jar.
He straightened out Ernie's roller skate.
He oiled Grover's squeaky wagon wheels.
He made a new seat for Herry's chair.
He put a new tab in Prairie Dawn's radio.

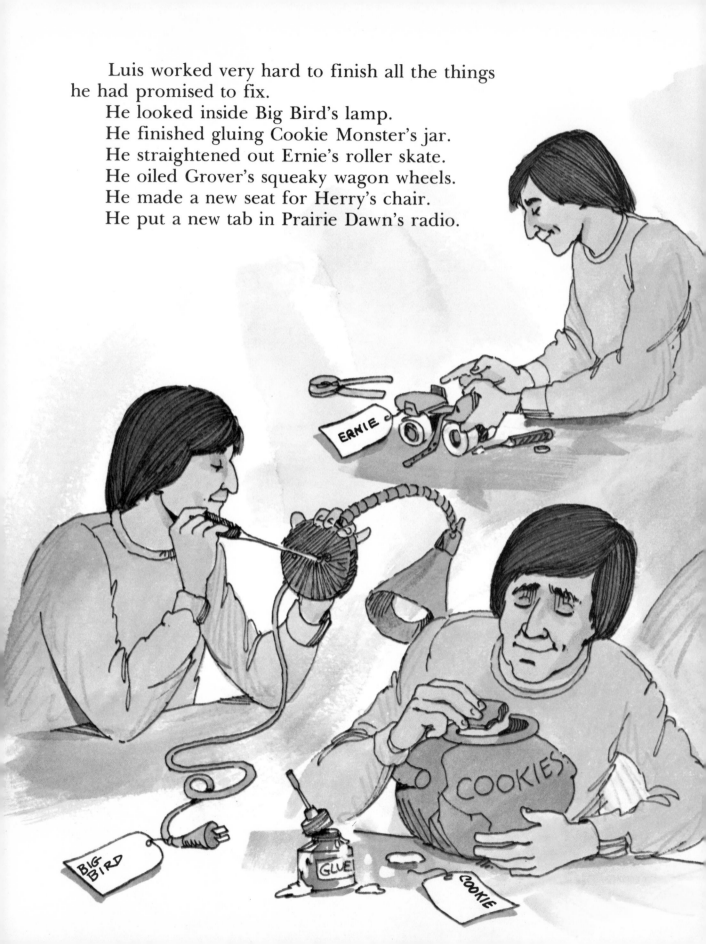

Just as Luis was all finished, Maria came back into the Fix-It Shop.

"Luis!" she said. "Why don't you stop working and go home? Don't you know how late it is?"

Luis sighed. "I've been trying all day to find the time to fix my clock, and now the day is over. Anyway, I think I have some visitors," he said, looking out the door.

Luis saw all his friends coming down the street.

"Thank you, Luis!" everyone said, trying out
all the things Luis had fixed.

"By the way, Big Bird," said Luis, "there wasn't anything
wrong with your lamp. I think you just forgot to plug it in."

Luis was glad he had fixed everything that was broken
on Sesame Street. "Tomorrow," he thought, "I'll be able
to fix my clock at last!"

ABCDEFG